A NOTE TO PARENTS

When your children are ready to "step into reading," giving them the right books is as crucial as giving them the right food to eat. **Step into Reading Books** and STAR WARS® **JEDI READERS** present exciting stories and information reinforced with lively, colorful illustrations that make learning to read fun, satisfying, and worthwhile. They are priced so that acquiring an entire library of them is affordable. And they are beginning readers with a difference—they're written on five levels.

Early Step into Reading Books are designed for brand-new readers, with large type and only one or two lines of very simple text per page. **Step 1 Books** feature the same easy-to-read type as the Early Step into Reading Books, but with more words per page. **Step 2 Books** are both longer and slightly more difficult, while **Step 3 Books** introduce readers to paragraphs and fully developed plot lines. **Step 4 Books** offer exciting fiction and nonfiction for the increasingly independent reader.

The grade levels assigned to the five steps—preschool through kindergarten for the Early Books, preschool through grade 1 for Step 1, grades 1 through 3 for Step 2, grades 2 through 3 for Step 3, and grades 2 through 4 for Step 4—are intended only as guides. Some children move through all five steps very rapidly; others climb the steps over a period of several years. Either way, these books will help your child "step into reading" in style!

www.randomhouse.com/kids
www.starwars.com

ISBN 0-375-80431-5 (trade) — ISBN 0-375-90431-X (lib. bdg.)

Printed in the United States of America March 2000   10 9 8 7 6 5 4 3 2 1

STEP INTO READING, RANDOM HOUSE and the Random House colophon are
registered trademarks and the Step into Reading colophon is a trademark of
Random House, Inc.

JEDI READERS

STAR WARS®

EPISODE I

ANAKIN'S PIT DROID

A Step 2 Book

by Justine and Ron Fontes
illustrated by Christopher Moroney

Random House
New York

LUCAS BOOKS

Today is Boonta Race Day.

Flags wave in the big arena.

Everyone cheers
for the Podrace pilots.

Many pilots will race today.

But only one will win.

Anakin works hard
on his Podracer.
He wants to win this race.
It is the biggest race
of his life!

It is a big race
for DUM-4, too.
DUM-4 is Anakin's pit droid.
Pit droids fix Podracers.

Pit droids are not very smart.

And they often
fight with each other.

But they work hard.

DUM-4 loves helping Anakin.

Before the race,
DUM-4 sees a Jedi
talking to Anakin.
The Jedi seems to know
that Anakin is worried
about winning the race.
"Just do your best,"
the Jedi says to Anakin.
"May the Force be with you."

Anakin is ready
to power up his engines.
But something is wrong
with his Podracer.
"Oh, no!" he cries.
The power plug is missing.
And the race
is about to begin!

Anakin calls to his pit droid.

"DUM-4," he says,

"find me a power plug!

Fast!"

DUM-4 runs to Gasgano's pit.

Gasgano is a Podrace pilot

with six limbs

and twenty-four fingers.

His pit is next to Anakin's.

"I will give you a power plug,"
Gasgano says.

"But first you must bring me
a thrust cone."

"Where can I get a thrust cone?"
asks DUM-4.

"From Sebulba," says Gasgano.

Gasgano points to Sebulba's pit.

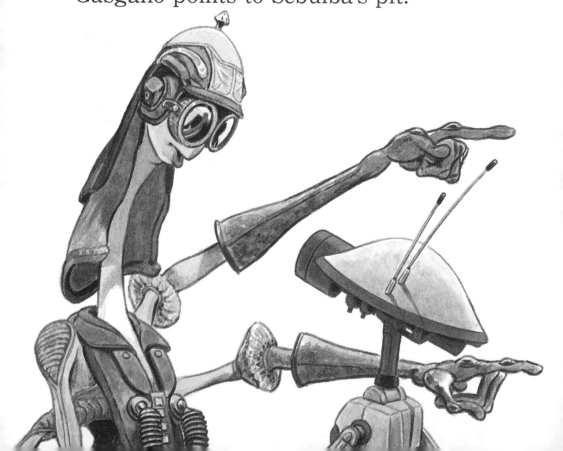

DUM-4 runs as fast as he can
to Sebulba's pit.

Sebulba is a mean Dug.
He always wins Podraces
by cheating
and playing dirty tricks.
"Hurry it up, bolt brains!"
Sebulba shouts
at his pit droids.
DUM-4 taps Sebulba
on the back.

The Dug spins around.
"What do you want?"
he yells angrily.
DUM-4 is so surprised
he folds up!

"I need a thrust cone," DUM-4 says,
unfolding himself.
Sebulba thinks for a moment.
"I will give you a thrust cone.
But first you must
take this message
to Jabba the Hutt.
And bring back his answer."
Jabba the Hutt is even meaner
than Sebulba!
But DUM-4 wants to help Anakin.

DUM-4 starts across the track.

Some Podracers are flying

practice laps.

Podracers fly very fast.

"Look out!" a pilot cries.

DUM-4 is almost run over!

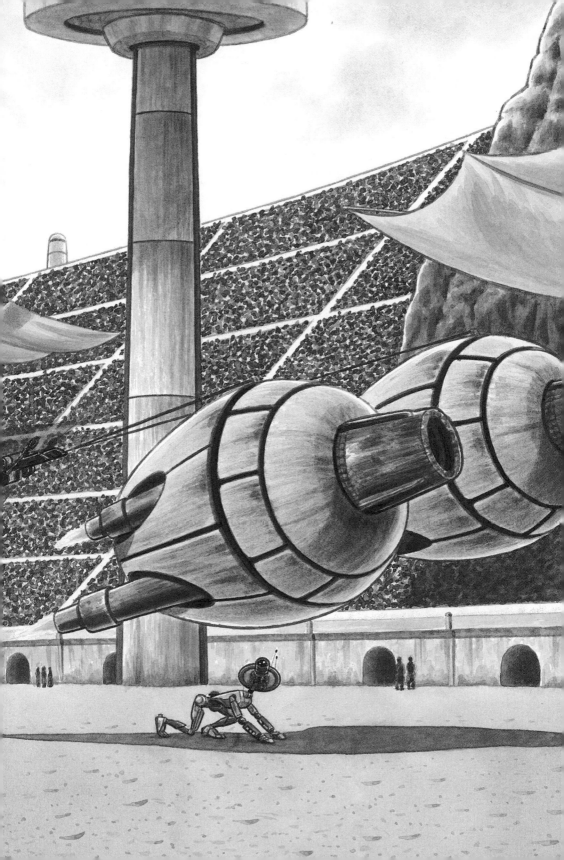

DUM-4 climbs

the steps to Jabba's seat.

He has almost reached the top.

But a pilot named Ody runs by

and bumps into him.

DUM-4 falls all the way

down the stairs!

DUM-4 starts climbing up again.

The steps go on and on!

At last he reaches Jabba.
The Hutt is big, green,
and slimy.
"Why does this pit droid
DARE to bother me?"
Jabba asks his helper,
Bib Fortuna.
"I do not know, master,"
says Bib.
"Perhaps we should
melt him down
for Podracer parts."

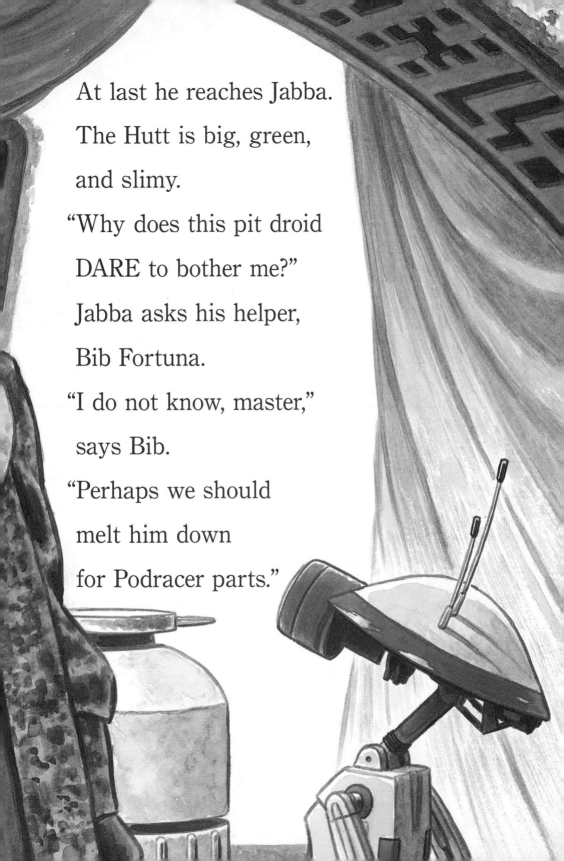

DUM-4's arm rattles
with fear as he holds out
Sebulba's note.
Jabba and Bib Fortuna
laugh at the little droid.
Bib takes the paper
and passes it to Jabba.

Jabba reads the note
with interest.
Then Jabba tells Bib
to write an answer
on the paper.

"Little pit droid!" shouts Jabba.

"Deliver my answer!"

DUM-4 takes the note,
and Jabba swishes
his big, fat tail.
DUM-4 flies through the air!
He falls down, down, down.

Clunk!

He lands on the racetrack!

Suddenly, the announcer
with two heads speaks.
"Find your seats, fans,"
says one head.
"The Boonta Race starts
in five minutes!"
says the other.

DUM-4 does not know what to do!

The race is going to start,

and Sebulba's pit is

far away!

Then he sees a Podracer

speeding by.

DUM-4 grabs

the back of the Podracer.

Wheeee!

The Podracer zooms DUM-4

back to Sebulba's pit.

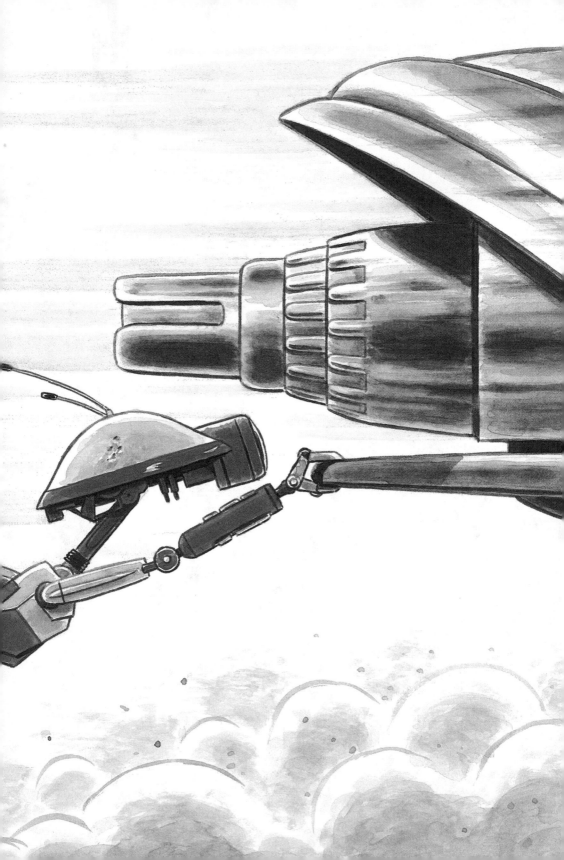

DUM-4 gives Sebulba
the note with Jabba's answer.
Sebulba nods
and gives DUM-4
the thrust cone.

DUM-4 races to Gasgano's pit.

He gives Gasgano

the thrust cone.

And Gasgano gives him

the power plug.

DUM-4 runs to Anakin's pit.

The race is about to begin!

He gives Anakin the power plug.

"Good job, DUM-4!"

says Anakin.

"You are just in time."

DUM-4 helps Anakin
put the power plug
into his Podracer.
Anakin starts the engines.
Whoosh!
They roar with power!

Anakin joins
the other Podrace pilots
at the starting line.
A gong sounds
for the race to begin.
Va-roooooooom!
All the Podracers take off
in a cloud of dust.
All except Anakin!

Anakin's engines
are not working!
DUM-4 is so upset
he can barely watch.
What will Anakin do?

Anakin remembers
the Jedi's words.
Just do your best.
Anakin flips the switches
and tries again.

The Podracer roars to life!
Anakin speeds after
the other Podracers.
He flies faster than ever
and quickly catches up.

Sebulba tries one of his
dirty tricks.
He rams his Podracer
into Anakin's.
But Anakin will not
give up!
He just flies faster!

Anakin does his best.

And he wins!

The crowd cheers!

DUM-4 jumps up and down.

He is happy because

he did his best, too.

He helped Anakin win.

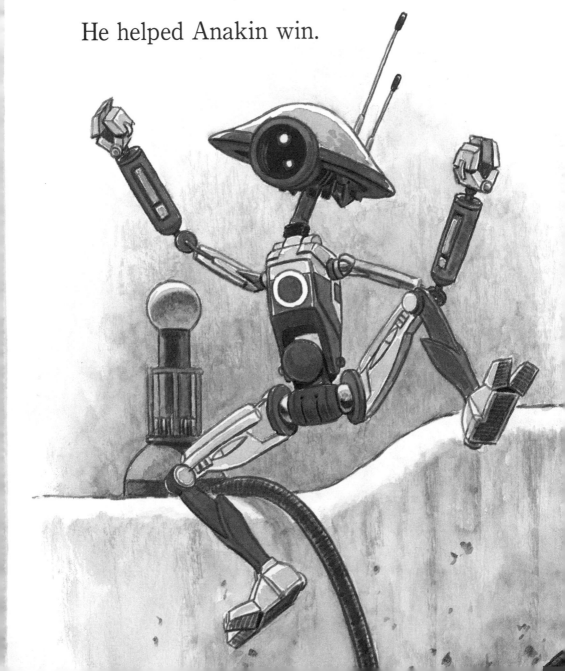

DUM-4 folds himself up.

He has earned a good rest.

Doing your best

can be very tiring!